Crazy Clothes

illustrated by Suçie Stevenson

ALADDIN BOOKS

Macmillan Publishing Company/*New York*   Maxwell Macmillan Canada/*Toronto*
Maxwell Macmillan International/*New York*   *Oxford*   *Singapore*   *Sydney*

Niki Yektai

Crazy Clothes

Aladdin Books
Macmillan Publishing Company
866 Third Avenue
New York, NY 10022

Maxwell Macmillan Canada, Inc.
1200 Eglinton Avenue East
Suite 200
Don Mills, Ontario M3C 3N1

Macmillan Publishing Company is part of the Maxwell Communication
Group of Companies.
Printed in the United States of America
10 9 8 7 6 5 4 3 2 1
The text of this book is set in 20 pt. Zapf Book.
The illustrations are watercolor.

Library of Congress Cataloging-in-Publication Data
Yektai, Niki.
Crazy clothes / Niki Yektai; illustrated by Suçie Stevenson.—1st Aladdin Books ed.
p.   cm.
Summary: When Patrick tries to show his mother how well he can dress himself, his
clothes become contrary and insist on going on the wrong parts of his body.
ISBN 0-689-71781-4
[1. Clothing and dress—Fiction.] I. Stevenson, Suçie. ill. II. Title.
PZ7.Y376Cr 1994
[E]—dc20   93-19738

For Nico Yektai,
who had a lot of crazy clothes
at one time
—N.Y.

For Emma and her Godzilla
—S.S.

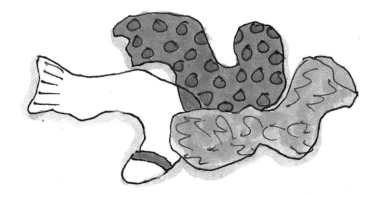

"Mommy, come here! Sit down!" said Patrick. "I want you to watch me. I'm going to get dressed all by myself."

"Good," said Mommy. "I'd love to watch. You're very grown up."
She sat on Patrick's bed.

Patrick took his pants from the drawer.
"Hey! Where do you think you're
going?" he said to his pants.

Patrick looked in the mirror. His pants were on his head.

"Oh, I get it," said Patrick to his pants. "You're tired of being pants.

You want to be a hat today. I think you make a great hat. Stay right where you are!"

Patrick took a sweater out of his drawer.

"Hold it! Have you gone crazy too?" Patrick asked his sweater.

Mommy said, "It looks like your
sweater has decided to be pants today."
"That's fine with me," said Patrick.
"I like these pants. They look terrific!"

"Get this straight!" said Patrick to
a white shirt he pulled out of the drawer.
"I'm the boss and I say you've got to be
a shirt today or else!"
Patrick put the shirt over his head.

"Help! I'm stuck!" said Patrick.
"I told you, shirt, NO FOOLING AROUND!"
The shirt would not come down over
his head.

Then Patrick had an idea. He ran over to Mommy and yelled, "BOOOOOOO!" Mommy jumped off the bed.
"Oh, dear! There's a ghost in the house!" cried Mommy.

Patrick laughed under the shirt. He pulled once more and it came down over his head.

"It's only me," he said.

"I won't bother with sleeves," said
Patrick. Mommy was looking at her watch.
  "I've got lots of work to do," she said.
  "I'll hurry," said Patrick. Mommy was
getting fidgety.

"Socks, you're next," said Patrick.
He opened a drawer. "Now, what'll I do?"
he asked. "Red socks—you want to
be picked to match my new red pants.
And blue socks—you want to be picked
to match my blue hat."

Patrick shrugged. "I'll pick one of each
and make you both happy," he said.

"You feel very warm and nice," exclaimed Patrick to his socks. "Forget about going on my feet. You are mittens! Great!"

"Which is which?"

"You don't know your left from your right," said Patrick to his shoes.

His right shoe was on his left foot and his left shoe was on his right foot.

"Let's see if I can walk....Yes, of course I can. Shoes, stay right where you are!"

"Now for the coat trick," said Patrick. "Look, Mom! My teacher taught me this." He laid his coat on the floor and put his arms in.

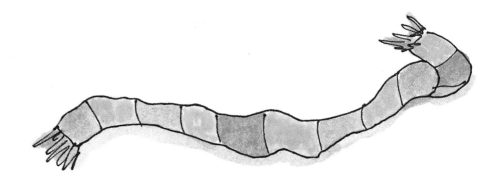

"Coat! *You're* playing a trick on me!" cried Patrick. "You've gone backwards!" Patrick looked in the mirror and laughed. But Mommy wasn't laughing at all.

"It was funny at first," said Mommy. "But now I'm beginning to think you're not grown up enough to dress yourself."

"I CAN TOO DRESS MYSELF!"
protested Patrick. "It's the *clothes*
that were fooling around. Now they'll
cooperate. Don't go away, Mommy! Close
your eyes and count to a hundred."

Mommy closed her eyes and
started counting. She was only at
eighty-eight when Patrick said,
"Open your eyes."

"Oh, Patrick!" said Mommy, clapping
her hands. "You dressed so fast!"

"Of course I can dress myself,"
explained Patrick. "Those clothes were
acting crazy. But they'll be good
from now on. I hope..."